Shlemiel Crooks

ANNA OLSWANGER

ILLUSTRATED BY

PAULA GOODMAN KOZ

Junebug Books
Montgomery

Junebug Books
P.O. Box 1588
Montgomery, AL 36102

Published in the United States by Junebug Books, an imprint of NewSouth, Inc., Montgomery, Alabama.

Library of Congress Cataloging-in-Publication Data

Olswanger, Anna, 1953–
Shlemiel crooks / Anna Olswanger; illustrated by Paula Goodman Koz.
p.   cm.
Based on a true incident in the lives of the author's great-grandparents.
Summary: Two crooks, following the inspiration of Pharaoh's ghost, fail to steal a precious shipment of
kosher wine from Israel and lose their horse and wagon in the process.
Society of Children's Book Writers & Illustrators Magazine Merit Award for Fiction, 1998.

ISBN 1-58838-165-X (alk. paper)
1. Jews–United States–History–20th century–Juvenile fiction. [1. Jews–United States–History–20th century–
Fiction. 2. St. Louis (Mo.)–History–20th century–Fiction. 3. Robbers and outlaws–Fiction. 4. Humorous stories.]
I. Goodman Koz, Paula, ill. II. Title.
PZ7.O522Shl 2005
[Fic]–dc22
2004030108

Printed in Korea by Pacifica Communications

An earlier version of "Shlemiel Crooks" appeared in *The Young Judaean Magazine* and won the
1998 Society of Children's Book Writers & Illustrators Magazine Merit Award for Fiction.

Acknowledgments: Matt Darrish, Dr. Walter Ehrlich, Rabbi Rafael Grossman, Dr. Nathan Kaganoff.
Special thanks to Tracy Massey, of Massey Camera Shop, Williamsburg, Virginia,
for the many painstaking hours spent scanning the art.

In memory of
Elias and Dora Olschwanger

In the middle of the night on a Thursday, two crooks—onions should grow in their navels—drove their horse and wagon to the saloon of Reb Elias Olschwanger at the corner of Fourteenth and Carr Streets in St. Louis. This didn't happen yesterday. It was 1919.

Reb Elias, you should know, didn't have a sit-down kind of saloon with men coming in to guzzle whiskey. Oh, no! Reb Elias had the kind of saloon with housewives—grandmas even—coming in to buy bottles of wine and brandy, unopened of course and strictly kosher, for the Jewish Sabbath. He was the only one in St. Louis selling kosher wines back then. Listen, he also sold kosher cognac—that's a kind of brandy—and mead, which is made out of honey and goes down easy. For the children, he kept in the back a barrel of pretzels with lots of thick salt on them.

Meanwhile, the two crooks—potatoes should sprout in their ears—were stealing crates of Passover wine shipped special that year to Reb Elias on a boat from the Land of Israel. Reb Elias paid a little more—okay, he paid a lot more—for that wine. Usually he was buying his Passover stock from the Manischewitz family in Cincinnati. But after Mr. Balfour—excuse me, Lord Balfour—a big politician in England, promised to make a home for the Jews in the Land of Israel, Reb Elias thought maybe they could use the extra business over there. The Jews swatting mosquitoes overseas shouldn't have only watery soup and a little goat's milk to drink.

So you won't worry he got his brains knocked out by those lousy crooks, I'll tell you that Reb Elias was sitting at a table in the synagogue three blocks down on Eleventh Street. He was keeping company with Perlmutter, the tailor; Birnbaum, the watchmaker; six dry goods men; and one rag man. This rag man, I'm pleased to say, later opened up a candy store and stayed put.

Reb Elias happened to be the leader of the Talmud Society at the synagogue. Every night he was sitting up late in the study room and sipping hot tea over a page of Talmud. He liked his tea plain, no sugar. That particular night, he was leading a discussion—okay, maybe it was more like an argument—about the first Passover when the Israelites got the boot out of Egypt.

Reb Elias was saying in a nice Yiddish that when the Israelites waved good-bye to Pharaoh in the middle of the Red Sea, they weren't exactly standing there empty-handed. They had managed to take a little something in the way of jewelry and clothing from the Egyptians. So over the years, certain people—Reb Elias wasn't mentioning names—kept trying to give the Jews a reputation for being swindlers.

By the way, you don't have to thank me, but what I'm giving you here is my personal translation from Reb Elias's Yiddish.

"And who do you think was worried sick about the Egyptians' reputation?" Reb Elias asked Perlmutter, Birnbaum, the six dry goods men, and the rag man. "I'll tell you. The Israelites! You take a look in the Talmud, you'll see that after a couple hundred years of slave labor, they went asking the Egyptians for a little back pay, in this case jewelry and clothes. That way, nobody should go around calling the

Egyptians slave drivers when it was Pharaoh they should be giving the bad name to."

Having set the record straight—the Jews were never swindlers—Reb Elias was taking a snooze. Listen, he wasn't exactly a spring chicken. In fact, he was an old man already, past seventy. So at 11 o'clock at night, he wouldn't have minded being at home in his bed above Resnik's grocery, a nice feather blanket up to his beard, and Mrs. Olschwanger snoring in her bed next to his.

Perlmutter, the tailor, leaned across the table. "You were listening, Birnbaum?" he asked. "You heard Reb Elias say that when the Jews told Pharaoh good-bye, nice knowing you, God let them take a little back pay from the Egyptians? Well, Birnbaum, what do you think the Jews were wandering around in for forty years? I'll tell you. They were wandering

around in nice linen skirts with pleats, very stylish, because they got their back pay in garments."

"Garments! Phooey!" sputtered Birnbaum, the watchmaker. "You were in the Other World maybe when Reb Elias told how the Jews got their back pay in jewelry? So for your information, they were wandering around in necklaces and bracelets, decorated with diamonds like you see on the face of a lady's nice wristwatch!"

Reb Elias meanwhile was busy sleeping like a log. He wasn't interrupting Perlmutter and Birnbaum— they should only have gone on enjoying themselves.

I'll let you in on something. Back when the Israelites were telling Pharaoh they'd be seeing him in the funny papers, you think it was only jewelry and clothing they were loading into saddle bags on camels? You think they weren't packing in a little something to eat on the way? The unleavened bread you probably heard about already, but according to my sources—which I'm keeping confidential, so don't even ask—plenty of dried grapes—okay, raisins—were going into those saddle bags from Pharaoh's own vineyards. How were the Israelites supposed to know they'd end up eating manna from heaven and dragging those raisins around the desert for forty years?

And where do you think the grapes came from that got squashed into the wine shipped to Reb Elias from the Land of Israel in 1919? I'll tell you: they came from seeds stuck inside

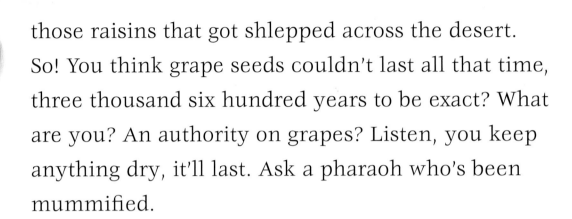

those raisins that got shlepped across the desert. So! You think grape seeds couldn't last all that time, three thousand six hundred years to be exact? What are you? An authority on grapes? Listen, you keep anything dry, it'll last. Ask a pharaoh who's been mummified.

Speaking of which, in case you haven't been reading the book of Exodus in the Bible lately, I'll remind you that the Pharaoh who was calling the shots during the first Passover wasn't exactly partial to the Israelites, never mind they built him two nice cities, Ramses and Pithom, which I'd like to point out nobody today bothers to mention in the same breath with the Jews. Not that I'm complaining. But you think this Pharaoh got finished off when he went chasing after the Israelites into the Red Sea? Ha! Listen to this: in 1919 Pharaoh was still sneaking around trying to pull one over on the Jews! He wasn't walking around in loose bandages like a mummy you see in the movies. Nobody was getting

a good look at him altogether because in plain words, he was a ghost. And such an operator! He reminded me of my cousin Shloime. You turn your back for one second, he's putting your cream-cheese-on-rye in his pocket to take home and enjoy maybe with a dill pickle.

So after more than three thousand years, this Pharaoh was still sore about losing his Israelite slaves. As soon as he got wind of Reb Elias's special shipment of wine from the Land of Israel, he came sniffing around to see if the wine smelled anything like the grapes off his vines. And with Reb Elias's luck, Pharaoh had a good nose.

So what did Pharaoh do? He hotfooted it down to the levee, the part of St. Louis where you wouldn't want to find yourself walking alone at night. He sidled up to a couple of crooks—they already did time in the workhouse for highway robbery. Pharaoh gave a little cough and mentioned to the crooks—they should die of heartburn—that it was the middle of the night and nobody was minding Reb Elias Olschwanger's saloon.

At first the crooks thought maybe they were hearing a fly buzz near their heads. They swatted at it a time or two and kept on talking about whether they should be betting their money on Pal Moore or Kid Regan in the bout coming up at the Coliseum. This got Pharaoh mad—maybe he didn't go in for boxing—and he started calling the crooks some not-nice names. Then they got the hint.

"Hey," one of them said, "I been hangin' around a saloon up on Fourteenth Street, givin' it the once-over . . ."

Before he got it out of his mouth good about Reb Elias's special shipment of Passover wine, the second crook was already out the door—his teeth should fall out except one, then he could have a toothache.

You know what they say, a lock is only for honest men, so don't look surprised when I tell you that a big chisel and hammer were sliding around the floor of the wagon the crooks hitched up to their horse. Those two lowlifes cut through the chain on Reb Elias's saloon door like it was made out of straw, and the next thing you know, they were dragging his crates of Passover wine out to the sidewalk.

What a sorrow! Do you know what happens if Jews don't have wine at the seder, the name the Passover meal goes by? I'll tell you. It means they don't get to fill up a wine glass special for the prophet Elijah, he should take a sip on his way to all the other seders. Elijah, by the way, is like Pharaoh in that you can't see him exactly, not to mention he's capable

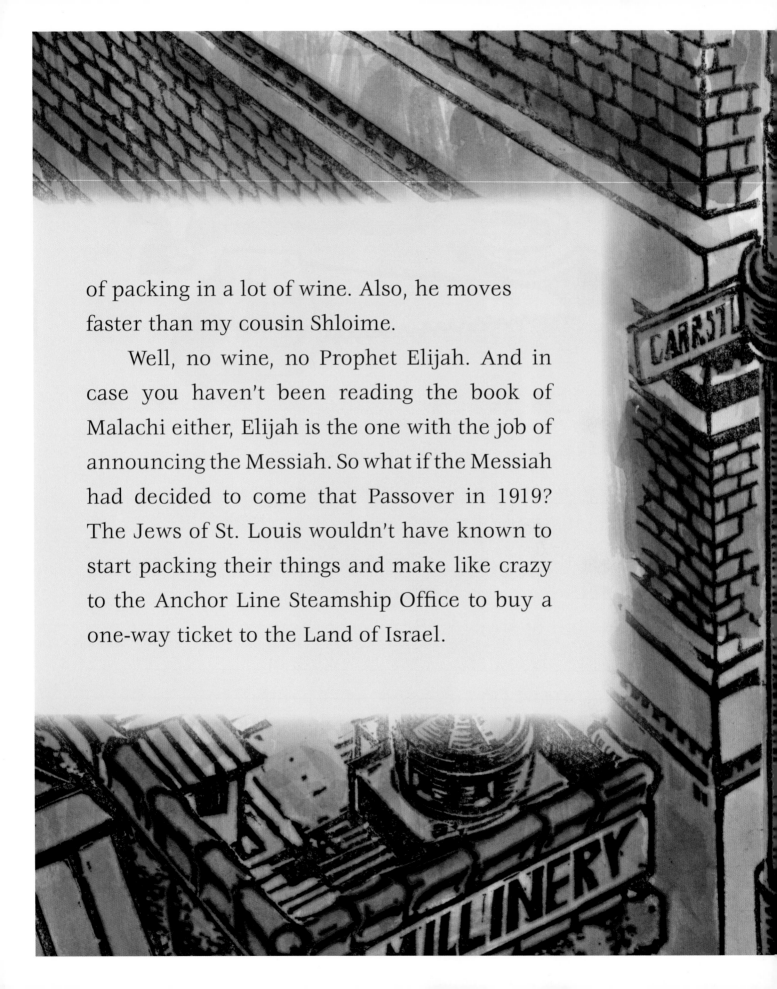

of packing in a lot of wine. Also, he moves faster than my cousin Shloime.

Well, no wine, no Prophet Elijah. And in case you haven't been reading the book of Malachi either, Elijah is the one with the job of announcing the Messiah. So what if the Messiah had decided to come that Passover in 1919? The Jews of St. Louis wouldn't have known to start packing their things and make like crazy to the Anchor Line Steamship Office to buy a one-way ticket to the Land of Israel.

Okay, those crooks—a trolley car should grow in their stomachs—were about to load Reb Elias's crates of wine into their wagon. Their horse was minding his own business, dreaming about some nice oats maybe, when he happened to get an eyeful of those bums standing over Reb Elias's wine. Maybe the horse felt put out, he wasn't getting a cut of the loot. Who knows? So in English even, plain like the nose on your face, he let out with, "Crooks! Crooks!"

Well, the two crooks gave a look to the horse, and then to each other, and not being exactly overstocked in the brains department, figured maybe the horse was letting out with a burp. Besides, who ever heard of a talking horse? Well, excuse me, but maybe the horses those crooks were used to being around just never had anything to say.

Also, you should know that the prophet Elijah wasn't standing around this whole time twiddling his thumbs. Maybe he put the horse up to it. You think only Pharaoh knew how to play a little dirty? The bottom line was, those crooks with sauerkraut for brains went on about their business of loading Reb Elias's wine into their wagon, never mind they had on their hands a talking horse.

By this time Mankel, who lived above Reb Elias's saloon, was sitting up in his bed and wondering what kind of shtuss was going on outside. He kept hearing somebody with a little indigestion call out, "Crooks! Crooks!"

When Mankel opened his window and saw Reb Elias's crates of Passover wine stacked one on top of the other, he let out with a shout you could hear on the other side of St. Louis. "Thieves! Gonifs! They're robbing my friend Reb Elias Olschwanger! What! They want to take the bread out of an old man's mouth? That kind of aggravation he and his wife, such a nice lady, need? Call the police already! Help! Gevalt!"

Mankel would have kept on rattling his teakettle all night, which is to say he would have kept on yackety-yacking at the top of his lungs, but Resnik across the street opened his window, and as soon as he saw those two rotten eggs about to

load Reb Elias's wine into their wagon, he fired his pistol into the air.

Hoo-ha! Mrs. Moskowitz, who lived with her little boy next door to Mankel, started screaming like the bedbugs were eating her alive. Let me tell you, a voice like a canary, she didn't have.

So with the horse calling out, "Crooks! Crooks!" and Mankel yackety-yacking at the top of his lungs, Resnik shooting his pistol, and Mrs. Moskowitz making like she was dying from the bedbugs, all the people in the neighborhood

were soon wide awake and shouting from their windows, "Gonifs! Gevalt!"

Such a tummel they were making! So what did Pharaoh think the people living around Fourteenth and Carr streets were going to do when they saw Reb Elias's Passover wine sitting in the middle of the sidewalk? Mind their own business and go back to sleep? Didn't he know that after thousands of years of being without a place to hang their hats, the Jews had learned a thing or two about sticking together?

The crooks—it was about time—got scared. How scared? I'll tell you. They ran away like their pants were on fire and left Reb Elias's wine sitting in the middle of the sidewalk, not to mention their horse and wagon in the street.

Ah-haa, those good-for-nothings ended up one horse and wagon poorer, which goes to show that if you spit up in the air, the spit's going to land on your own face.

Meanwhile, Reb Elias was walking up Carr Street from the synagogue, wondering what all the mish-mosh in front of his saloon was about. When he got to the corner, he heard the news that he was robbed, but not exactly. He promised Mrs. Moskowitz's little boy a pretzel, he should run down to Eleventh Street and ask the editor at *The Jewish Record*—he was up all hours—to print this ad, which I'm nice enough to translate for you into English:

ELIAS OLSCHWANGER

wants to thank all his friends
on Fourteenth and Carr streets who stopped the
no-good crooks from stealing his wine.

Don't worry, he's still got a fine stock of
full and half-bottles of

LAND OF ISRAEL WINE AND
BRANDIES FOR PASSOVER.

Also, now he's delivering in a horse and wagon, you shouldn't
have to come to him, you're so busy.

Only, in case the shlemiel crooks come back for the horse
and wagon, you could order now maybe?

E. Olschwanger
Liquor Company
1028 North 14th Stre

So it shouldn't be a shock, I'm telling you now that those two crooks—worms should hold a wedding in their bellies—were never caught, not that the police didn't search high and low. Who knows? Maybe Pharaoh did a vanishing act with them, same as my cousin Shloime does with my cream-cheese-on-rye sandwiches.

Reb Elias got to keep the talking horse, only afterwards nobody heard it so much as burp. That just proves that a horse doesn't open its mouth unless it's got something to say. I know a few people, they should follow the same advice. ◼

Postscript

Anna Olswanger never knew her great-grandparents Elias and Dora Olschwanger, not even their names, until 1982. That was the year she made the first of several trips to St. Louis to research her family tree.

With the help of relatives she had never met and St. Louis historians, she located a number of newspaper articles that mentioned her great-grandfather "Reb Elias Olschwanger." The following articles became the basis for *Shlemiel Crooks*:

From the *St. Louis Jewish Record,* February 15, 1918:

אליהו אלשוואנגער

ווינשט באקאנט צו מאכען צו אללע זיינע פריינדע אז ער האט א פיינעם

אונד גרויסער סטאק פון נאנצע און האלבע באטעלס

כרמל ווינען און קאניאקס

אויך האט ער אויסגעקויפט א גרויסען סטאק פון

מאנישעוויץ פון סינסינעטי

קאליפארני ברענדי, שליוואוויץ און ווינען

אויך פסח'דיגע מעד

און וועט עס פערקויפען אויף מעסינע פרייזען.

קומט און בעזארגט אייך בעצייטענס בעפאר דעם ראש.

אליהו אלשוואנגער 1028 נ. 14טע

טעלעפאן סענטראל 8135 אר

Eliyahu Olschwanger

wishes to make known to all his friends

that he has a fine and

large stock of full and half-bottles of

Carmel wines and cognacs.

He has also purchased a large stock of

Manischewitz from Cincinnati,

California brandy,

slivowitz, and wines, also pesach'dik mead.

And it will be sold at reasonable prices.

Come and order in time before the rush.

Eliyahu Olschwanger, 1028 N. 14th,

Telephone Central 8135-AR.

From the *St. Louis Jewish Record*, February 21, 1919:

ר' אליהו אלשוואנגער
שיער ניט בעגנב'ט

שלימזלדינע גנבים, זייער ארבייט איז
ניט געלונגען. לעצטען דאנערשטאג אום
3 אזהר ביי נאכט זיינען זיך אייניגע ש־
וואַרצע צו געפאהרען צום סאלון פון ר'
אליהו אלשוואנגער, קאר. 14טע און קארר
סטס.. זיי האבען אויף געעפענט דעם סא־
לון און ארויס גענומען א פאאר פעסלאך
מיט ברענדי און ביער. מר. מענקעל
וואס וואהנט אויף דעם צווייטען פלאאר
דערהערענדיג וואס טהוט זיך אין סאלון,
האָט געעפענט די פענסטער און אָנגעפאַנ־
גען שרייען פיר הילף. בנימין רעזניק, פון
1329 קארר סט. דער הערענדיג די געש־
רייען האָט ער דורך דעם פענסטער אַרויס
געשאָסען פון זיין רעוואלווער. די חברה
גנבים האָבען זיך דערשראקען און איבער
גילאזם אלעם, אפילו זייער אייגענעם
פערד און וואגען און אנטלאפען. פאלים
זיינען באלד אָנגעקומען און האָבען אלעם
פערנומען אין דעם פאליס סטיישאָן.

Reb Eliyahu Olschwanger Almost Robbed

Shlimazel crooks, their work was unsuccessful. Last Thursday at 3:00 a.m. in the middle of the night, several men drove to the saloon of Reb Eliyahu Olschwanger at the corner of 14th and Carr streets. They opened the saloon and removed several barrels of brandy and beer. Mr. Mankel who lives on the second floor, upon hearing what was going on in the saloon, opened the window and began shouting for help. Benjamin Resnik from 1329 Carr Street, hearing the shouting, shot his revolver from his window. The band of crooks got scared and left everything, including their own horse and wagon and ran away. Police immediately came and took everything to the police station.